Achoo Island

Nostril
Mount

astle Isle

Nose Cape

Snotville

Piranha Lake

To my little pirate, Leo.

Alicia Acosta

With love to all the kids with runny noses.

Mónica Carretero

The Big Booger Battle
Little Captain Jack Series

© Text: Alicia Acosta, 2019
© Illustrations: Mónica Carretero, 2019
© Edition: NubeOcho, 2019
www.nubeocho.com · hello@nubeocho.com

Original title: *La isla de los mocos*
English translation: Céline Siret
Text editing: Eva Burke, Rebecca Packard and Laura Fielden

Distributed in the United States by
Consortium Book Sales & Distribution

First edition: november 2019
ISBN: 978-84-17123-91-8
Legal deposit: M-39097-2018

Printed in Portugal.

THE BIG BOOGER BATTLE

Alicia Acosta   Mónica Carretero

nubeOCHO

Once upon a time there was a pirate so little, so **very little**, that everybody called him **Little Captain Jack**.

One day he was looking through his spyglass when he saw a **bizarre bottle** floating in the water.

Little Captain Jack managed to grab the bottle.
There was a **message** inside that read,

*"Help! I'm on Achoo Island.
If you don't know where it is, go toward Hiss Island,
and you will find it halfway there."*

Little Captain Jack and his crew set sail for **Achoo Island,** but when they disembarked, they were met with quite a surprise! The residents were **walking noses** in all shapes and sizes: big, small, flat, sharp and round...

As soon as they saw Little Captain Jack's crew, the noses started attacking them with... **Achoo!** Sneezes and snot! **Achoo!** Snot and boogers! **Achoo!**

There was green snot everywhere.

The message had been a **trap!!**

The crew fled, taking cover and dodging the disgusting boogers. Little Captain Jack tried not to be stepped on by anyone by yelling his **famous ditty,**

*"Careful now,
watch your back,
here comes Little Captain Jack!"*

While they were looking for cover, suddenly a huge **clown nose** came up behind Little Captain Jack, and **achoo!** Little Captain Jack was completely covered in the **greenest of boogers**.

Splat!!!

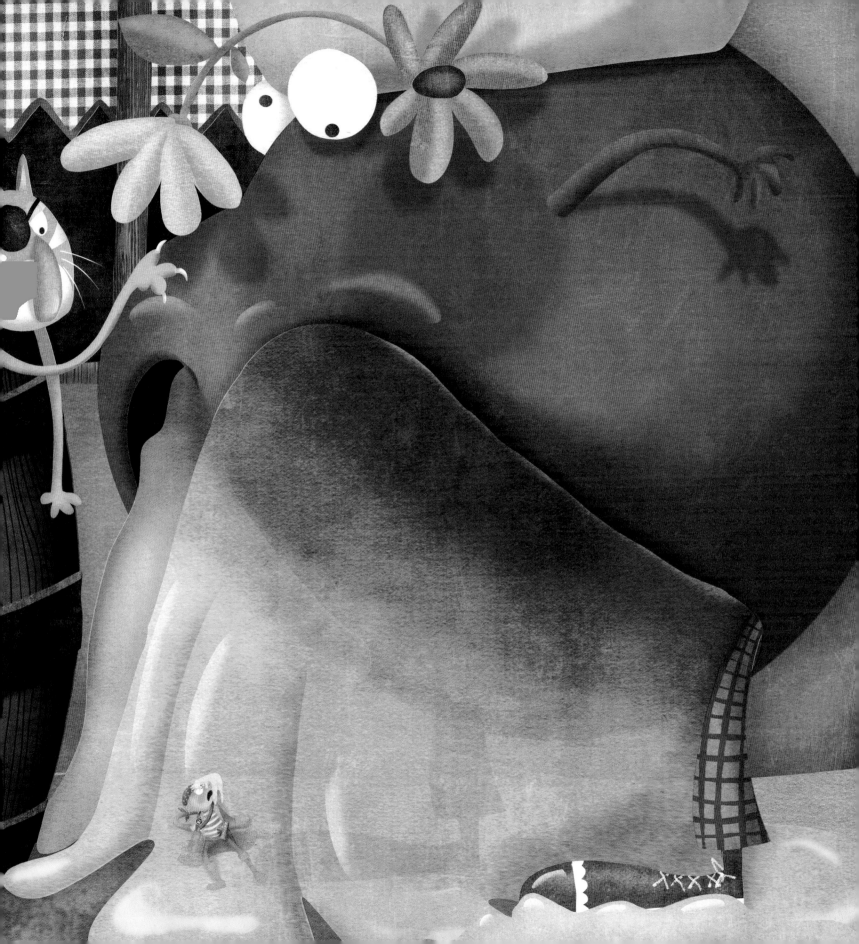

"Ewww!"
The crew quickly rescued their captain from the **mountain of snot** and fled to the boat.

They **bathed** him with care, **tucked him** in bed and gave him **hot soup**.

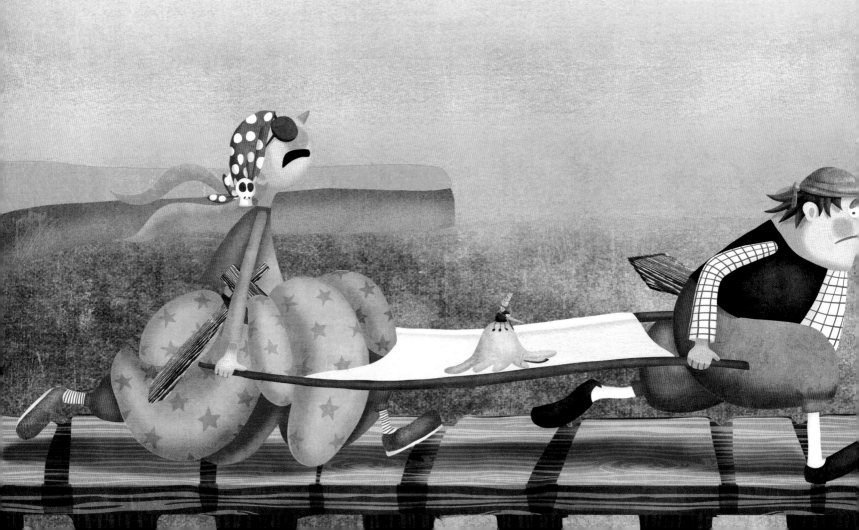

At daybreak, Little Captain Jack woke up with a **weird cold.** When he sneezed, it wasn't snot that came out of his nose... but **soap bubbles! Achoo!** Hundreds of soap bubbles started to fill the cabin.

When the crew saw the bubbles, they started to **jump** and **play** with them. But **Leo**, Little Captain Jack's loyal friend, was **swept away** by one of the bubbles!

Luckily, the crew managed to rescue him before he reached the **clouds!**

The next day, Little Captain Jack woke up to the sound of swords clashing. **Badlock**, a bad pirate, **as bad as they come**, had boarded the ship, and a **great battle** had started.

But when Little Captain Jack went to get his sword, he started sneezing again. Achooo! This time, out of his nose came **confetti!**

"**What a party!**" all the pirates thought. The fighting stopped and they all got out their instruments. They played music and everybody danced and sang along.

Little Captain Jack's crew hoped that the next day he would feel better, but when they woke up, their captain suddenly started sneezing again. This time it was **popcorn** flying out of his nose!

"**Outdoor cinema!**" the pirates cheered as they cleared the deck to watch a movie.

After a while though, Little Captain Jack and his crew started to get a bit fed up with the **bizarre cold**. They decided to go back to Achoo Island to see if the noses would give Little Captain Jack an antidote. But what could they offer in exchange? **Gold? Jewels? Gemstones?**

"I have an idea!" Little Captain Jack said.

They quickly went to the **closest harbor**, brought onboard a **gigantic chest** and set sail again for Achoo Island.

When Little Captain Jack and his crew
opened the chest, the noses from Achoo Island
clapped happily and **celebrated**. The chest was
filled with **tons of hankies!**
They would be able to **clean their boogers** for the
rest of their lives!

The noses were delighted with the gift, and they gave Little Captain Jack the **antidote**. He finally felt better and learned an **important lesson**:

"Make sure you have a hanky in your hand if you travel to Booger Land."

SHARK ISLANDS

Tiny Island

Hiss Island

Skull Islet

N

NW

NE

W

E

SW

SE

S